PUFFIN BOOKS

THE PUFFIN BOOK O

All poetry is magic. Charles
thology includes not only inca
poems about elves, changelin
mermaids, but it also introduc
and magic of the natural world and everyday life – those
happenings that perhaps we take for granted. Mist and
wind, sun and moon, these and other natural phenomena
are charged with a magic close to our senses, our minds
and imaginations. Magic is not just a faraway thing of
the past but is also to be discovered here, today. But
wherever one finds magic, one thing seems certain: the
language of magic always has been – and always must
be – the language of poetry.

This selection of magic verse extends from the songs
of primitive societies and Anglo-Saxon verses to Shakespeare, Ben Jonson, Blake, Emily Brontë, Robert Burns,
W. S. Gilbert, Kipling, W. B. Yeats, Thomas Hardy,
Robert Frost, W. H. Auden, John Betjeman and dozens
of others down to the work of such younger poets as
Brian Patten and Jeni Couzyn.

The editor, Charles Causley, is a distinguished poet
and his books of verse for children include *Figgie Hobbin*,
Figure of 8 and *The Tail of the Trinosaur*.

Barbara Świderska's illustrations visually echo the
spell-binding quality of the poems in this magical
collection.

Other collections from Charles Causley

EARLY IN THE MORNING
FIGGIE HOBBIN
THE PUFFIN BOOK OF SALT-SEA VERSE
THE SUN, DANCING
THE TAIL OF THE TRINOSAUR

THE PUFFIN BOOK OF
MAGIC VERSE

Chosen and Introduced
by
Charles Causley

Illustrated by
Barbara Świderska

PUFFIN BOOKS

PUFFIN BOOKS

Published by the Penguin Group
Penguin Books Ltd, 27 Wrights Lane, London W8 5TZ, England
Penguin Books USA Inc., 375 Hudson Street, New York, New York 10014, USA
Penguin Books Australia Ltd, Ringwood, Victoria, Australia
Penguin Books Canada Ltd, 10 Alcorn Avenue, Toronto, Ontario, Canada M4V 3B2
Penguin Books (NZ) Ltd, 182–190 Wairau Road, Auckland 10, New Zealand

Penguin Books Ltd, Registered Offices: Harmondsworth, Middlesex, England

First published 1974
13 15 17 19 20 18 16 14

This collection copyright © Charles Causley, 1974
Illustrations copyright © Penguin Books Ltd, 1974
All rights reserved

Printed in England by Clays Ltd, St Ives plc
Set in Monotype Ehrhardt

CONTENTS

Introduction   15

CHARMS AND SPELLS

Charm for St Valentine's Eve *Anonymous*   23
Charm for a Lover *Anonymous*   23
Love-Charm Songs *Anonymous*   24
Charm on Seeing a Pisky *Anonymous*   24
Charme *Robert Herrick*   25
Charme *Robert Herrick*   25
Charm against a Magpie *Anonymous*   26
Charme *Robert Herrick*   26
Charm against an Egg-Boat *Anonymous*   27
Charm for a Wart *Anonymous*   27
'The Soul is the Breath in your Body' *Jeni Couzyn*   28
Charme for Stables *Robert Herrick*   29
Charm for a Thorn-Prick *Anonymous*   30

CONTENTS

Charm for an Adder Bite *Anonymous* — 30

Rattlesnake Ceremony Song *Anonymous* — 31

Magic Song for Him who wishes to Live *Anonymous* — 32

Charm for the Toothache *Anonymous* — 32

Charm to Stanch Bleeding *Anonymous* — 33

Charm for a Burn or Scald *Anonymous* — 33

Charm for Wildfire *Anonymous* — 34

Charm *Anonymous, translated from the Polish by Jerzy Peterkiewicz and Burns Singer* — 34

Curing Song *Anonymous* — 35

West Wind to the Bairn *Anonymous* — 35

Song to bring Fair Weather *Anonymous* — 36

The Rogery Birds *Mary Gilmore* — 36

Rain Song *Anonymous* — 38

Plaint against the Fog *Anonymous* — 39

Aztec Song *Anonymous, translated by Lowell Dunham* — 39

The Soldier Campion *W. S. Graham* — 40

Two or Three Posies *John Keats* — 41

Carve her Name *Michael Baldwin* — 42

Struthill Well *Anonymous* — 42

This is a Rune I have heard a Tree Say *George Barker* — 43

The Song at the Well *George Peele* — 44

Amergin's Charm *Robert Graves* — 45

Invocation of a Poet Seeking Inspiration *Anonymous* — 46

On a Midsummer Eve *Thomas Hardy* — 46

The Night-Piece, to Julia *Robert Herrick* — 47

Spell of Creation *Kathleen Raine* — 48

An Invocation *Samuel Taylor Coleridge* — 49

The Faery Beam Upon You *Ben Jonson* — 50

Upon that Night, when Fairies Light *Robert Burns* — 51

Spells *James Reeves* — 53

White Witchcraft *Robert Browning*   54

The Charm *Padraic Colum*   55

CURSES

A Spell to Destroy Life *Anonymous*   59

St Newlina's Staff *Anonymous*   60

Charm for Striking Fear into a Tiger and Hardening One's Own Heart *Anonymous*   61

Glaucopis *Richard Hughes*   62

Long John Brown & Little Mary Bell *William Blake*   63

Her Strong Enchantments Failing *A. E. Housman*   64

La Belle Dame sans Merci *John Keats*   64

The Man in the Wilderness *Anonymous*   67

There she Weaves by Night and Day *Alfred, Lord Tennyson*   67

Noble Sisters *Christina Rossetti*   69

WARLOCKS, WITCHES AND WIZARDS

The Egg-Shell *Rudyard Kipling*   73

Hallowe'en *Leonard Clark*   74

All Hail, Great Master! *William Shakespeare*   75

The Warden *Stevie Smith*   76

The Witch *Walter de la Mare*   77

When Shall We Three Meet Again *William Shakespeare*   79

Dame Hickory *Walter de la Mare*   80

Thrice the Brinded Cat hath Mew'd *William Shakespeare*   81

The Hags' Song *Ben Jonson*   82

Oh! my name is John Wellington Wells *W. S. Gilbert*   85

The Great Nemo *Osbert Sitwell*   87

CONTENTS

CHANGELINGS

Hapless *Walter de la Mare* 91
The Stolen Child *W. B. Yeats* 92
The Three Beggars *Walter de la Mare* 94
The Changeling *Shirley Toulson* 96

GHOSTS AND HAUNTINGS

Song of Two Ghosts *Anonymous* 101
Old Mother Laidinwool *Rudyard Kipling* 101
The Strange Visitor *Anonymous* 103
Colonel Fazackerley *Charles Causley* 105
A Boy's Friend *Roy Fuller* 107
The Secret Brother *Elizabeth Jennings* 108
Dicky *Robert Graves* 109
The Knight's Ghost *Anonymous* 111
Lord Cozens Hardy *John Betjeman* 114
The Youth with the Red-Gold Hair *Edith Sitwell* 115
Shadwell Stair *Wilfred Owen* 116
City *John Betjeman* 116
Sally Simpkin's Lament *Thomas Hood* 117
The Spunky *Anonymous* 118
The Glimpse *Thomas Hardy* 120
The Ghost *Patricia Beer* 121
The Ballad of Keith of Ravelston *Sydney Dobell* 122
At Home *Christina Rossetti* 124
Sweet William's Ghost *Anonymous* 125
The Phantom-Lover *Thomas Lovell Beddoes* 128
The Ghosts' High Noon *W. S. Gilbert* 129
The Great Auk's Ghost *Ralph Hodgson* 130

CONTENTS

ENCHANTMENTS

The Totem Pole *Mary Gilmore* 133
Twelve Men's Moor *D. M. Thomas* 133
Right Cheek! Left Cheek! *Anonymous* 134
St Levan's Prophecy *Anonymous* 134
Crickstone *D. M. Thomas* 135
The Well of St Keyne *Richard Carew* 136
An Old and Crumbling Parapet *Mervyn Peake* 137
The Chough *John Heath-Stubbs* 138
Then Quickly Rose Sir Bedivere *Alfred, Lord Tennyson* 139
Robin Song *Ted Hughes* 140
The Scarecrow in the Schoolmaster's Oats
  George Mackay Brown 141
Song for the Spinning Wheel *William Wordsworth* 142
Harp of Wild and Dream-Like Strain *Emily Brontë* 143
Frutta Di Mare *Geoffrey Scott* 144
O Weary Lady, Geraldine *Samuel Taylor Coleridge* 145
Ardevora Veor *A. L. Rowse* 146
House Fear *Robert Frost* 148
Voices *Frances Bellerby* 149
Drowned, Sir, Drowned Men the Lot of Them!
  Thomas Blackburn 150
Rhyme for Children *Elizabeth Jennings* 152
I would Sing Songs *Anonymous, translated from the
  Polish by Jerzy Peterkiewicz and Burns Singer* 153

DWARFS, GIANTS, OGRES AND DEMONS

Wee Willie Gray *Robert Burns* 157
The Wee Wee Man *Anonymous* 158

CONTENTS

On Some Ghostly Companions at a Spa
Robert Louis Stevenson   160
In the Orchard *James Stephens*   161
Song of the Ogres *W. H. Auden*   162
Cold Lies the Dew *Anonymous*   163
The Deil's Awa wi' th' Exciseman *Robert Burns*   164
The Start of a Memorable Holiday *Roy Fuller*   165

EVENTS STRANGE AND FAMILIAR

The Three Singing Birds *James Reeves*   169
Cuckoo Song *Rudyard Kipling*   170
A Rare and Miraculous Case *Anonymous, translated from
the Spanish by W. S. Merwin*   172
The Seven Sisters *William Wordsworth*   174
A Small Dragon *Brian Patten*   176
The Serpent *Theodore Roethke*   177
The Roc *Edward Lowbury*   178
Vision of Belshazzar *George Gordon, Lord Byron*   179
The Cap and Bells *W. B. Yeats*   180
Up on the Downs *John Masefield*   182
Silent is the House – All are Laid Asleep *Emily Brontë*   183
Ends Meet *Frances Bellerby*   184
I saw a Strange Creature *Anonymous, translated from the
Anglo-Saxon* by *Kevin Crossley-Holland*   185
Song *Samuel Taylor Coleridge*   186
Windy Nights *Robert Louis Stevenson*   187
Kingdom of Mist *Edward Storey*   188
Stones *Leslie Norris*   189
Tom Bone *Charles Causley*   190
Check *James Stephens*   191

CONTENTS

SALT WATER SPIRITS, FRESH WATER SPIRITS

The Sailor Boy *Alfred, Lord Tennyson*   195
The Reverend Arbuthnot-Armitage-Brown
  George Barker   196
The Eddystone Light *Anonymous*   197
The Isles of Jessamy *Christopher Logue*   198
Count Arnaldos *Anonymous, translated from the Spanish*
  by W. S. Merwin   199
Glaucus *David Wright*   200
Sabrina Fair *John Milton*   201
Sabrina's Song *John Milton*   201
Cologne *Samuel Taylor Coleridge*   202

CREATURES OF EARTH AND AIR

The Crackling Twig *James Stephens*   205
Nan's Song *Maurice Carpenter*   206
The Tree *Andrew Young*   207
The Soldan's Song *Edith Sitwell*   208
Overheard on a Saltmarsh *Harold Monro*   209
O here it is! And there it is! *Mervyn Peake*   210
The Ancient Elf *James Stephens*   211
Fairy Story *Stevie Smith*   212
This is Mab, the Mistress-Fairy *Ben Jonson*   213
Fairy's Song *John Keats*   214
Wine of the Fairies *Percy Bysshe Shelley*   215
Ariel's Song *William Shakespeare*   215
From the Forests and Highlands *Percy Bysshe Shelley*   216
Song *John Milton*   216
The Fairy Queen *Anonymous*   217

CONTENTS

INTRODUCTION

ALL poetry is magic. It is a spell against insensitivity, failure of imagination, ignorance, and barbarism. The way that a good poem 'works' on a reader is as mysterious, as hard to explain, as the possible working of a charm or spell. A poem is much more than a mere arrangement of words on paper, or on the tongue. Its hints, suggestions, the echoes it sets off in the mind, and its omissions (what a poet decides to leave out is often just as important as what he puts in) all join up with the reader's thoughts and feelings and make a kind of magical union.

When he writes his poem, the poet is careful to make a space, a carefully unspecified area (you can't see it with the naked eye), which can be occupied by the mind and heart and imagination of the reader. Not, of course, that the poet is conscious of his audience when he is writing. At that time, he is both writer and reader, and the poem is for himself alone. Yet in just such a way, one imagines, the witches, wise ones, or 'pellers' as we sometimes call them in Cornwall, composed their spells in ways they hoped would be most successful.

The first poem was probably an incantation chanted in a cave against an imagined or real human enemy, or to help the hunter bring down his prey. It may have been made up of rhythmic grunts and cries (the original 'sound' poem) before the development of words as we know them today. The first magician, then, seems to have been also the first poet. Certainly, very many poets, at some stage or other in their writing lives, have been interested in writing poems with some kind of 'magical' theme.

Even in a scientific age, when people are more enlightened about such matters, the interest in magic continues. For magic has, at its core, a mystery. It is intensely personal; and no two people seem to have the same view about what the mystery may 'mean'.

So it is that we find a poet who was as much of his own age as W. H. Auden writing about ogres.

> Little fellow, you're amusing,
> Stop before you end by losing
> Your shirt:
> Run along to Mother, Gus,
> Those who interfere with us
> Get hurt.   (*page 162*)

Auden's ogres may not have been the giants of fairy-stories, but twentieth-century monsters of intolerance, greed, and suspicion. It is important to notice, all the same, that though this is a poem of menace, it is not a menacing poem. It is a poem of hope. It is, among other things, a sharp warning as to what may happen if we relax our watchfulness on the preservation of liberty.

Beneath the thin modern skin of life, beliefs in magic lie lightly sleeping, and are still very much alive. These folk-memories of our long crawl out of the prehistoric cave into the sun of reason will awaken easily. Who, for instance, has never instinctively touched wood for luck? Or not thrown a little